WELCOME TO PASSPORT TO READING

A beginning reader's ticket to a brand-new world!

Every book in this program is designed to build read-along and read-alone skills, level by level, through engaging and enriching stories. As the reader turns each page, he or she will become more confident with new vocabulary, sight words, and comprehension.

These PASSPORT TO READING levels will help you choose the perfect book for every reader.

READING TOGETHER
Read short words in simple sentence structures together to begin a reader's journey.

READING OUT LOUD
Encourage developing readers to sound out words in more complex stories with simple vocabulary.

READING INDEPENDENTLY
Newly independent readers gain confidence reading more complex sentences with higher word counts.

READY TO READ MORE
Readers prepare for chapter books with fewer illustrations and longer paragraphs.

This book features sight words from the educator-supported Dolch Sight Words List. This encourages the reader to recognize commonly used vocabulary words, increasing reading speed and fluency.

For more information, please visit www.passporttoreadingbooks.com.

Enjoy the journey!

Little, Brown and Company

Hachette Book Group
1290 Avenue of the Americas, New York, NY 10104
Visit our website at www.lb-kids.com

Little, Brown and Company is a division of Hachette Book Group, Inc.
The Little, Brown name and logo are trademarks of Hachette Book Group, Inc.

The publisher is not responsible for websites (or their content) that are not owned by the publisher.

First Edition: June 2013

ISBN 978-0-316-22830-5

Library of Congress Control Number: 2012947180

10 9 8 7 6

CWM

Printed in the U.S.A.

Passport to Reading titles are leveled by independent reviewers applying the standards developed by Irene Fountas and Gay Su Pinnell in *Matching Books to Readers: Using Leveled Books in Guided Reading*, Heinemann, 1999.

LICENSED BY:

Meet Heatwave the Fire-Bot

Adapted by Lisa Shea

Based on the episode
"Flobsters on Parade" written by
Brian Hohlfeld

LITTLE, BROWN AND COMPANY
New York Boston

Attention, Rescue Bots fans!

Look for these items when you read this book.

Can you spot them all?

FIRE TRUCK

LOBSTER

BALLOON

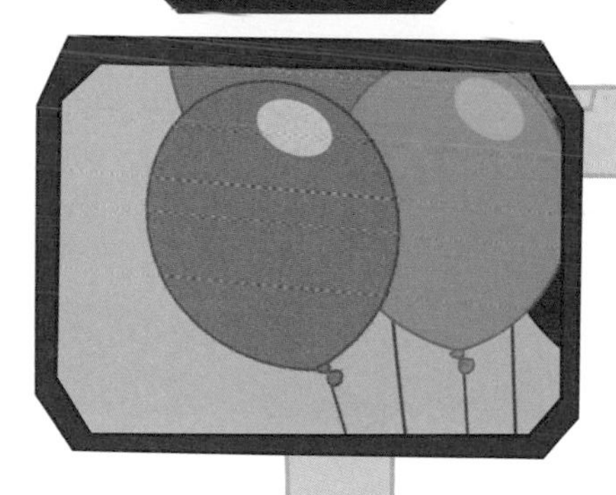

TELEVISION

I am Heatwave.
I am the team leader
of a special group
called the Rescue Bots.

Optimus Prime gave us a mission
to serve and protect humans.
My team members are
Chase, Boulder, and Blades.

I change into a fire truck
and work with a human
named Kade.
Kade knows my secret.

My secret is that I am an alien.
All the Rescue Bots are aliens.
We pretend to be
Earth robots to fit in.

The town prepares for a parade.
Doc Greene fills a big balloon.
The balloon is shaped like a lobster.
Doc gets tangled up in a string
and floats away!

I know what to do.

My ladder goes up in the air.

Kade climbs up.

Together, we save Doc Greene!

Doc and his daughter Francine
thank Kade but not me!

Doc thinks I am a normal robot
and I do not have feelings.
That makes me mad.
I am not just a robot.

The next day,

our friend Cody teaches us a game.

It is called Simon Says.

"Simon says, lift your arms,"

Cody calls out.

We lift our arms.

"Lift your left leg," Cody says.
Blades and Boulder lift their legs.
"He did not say 'Simon says,'"
Chase tells them.

“That is right, Chase,” says Cody.
“Remember to do only
what your humans tell you to do.”
If we follow that rule,
we will seem like Earth robots.

The Rescue Bots are going to march
in the parade.
We will pretend to be Earth robots.
I do not want to pretend.
"I will stay home," I say.

Cody tells me that
kids love to climb on fire trucks.
“One more reason not to go,” I say.
“Human children are sticky!”

Chief Burns arrives to take
the Rescue Bots to the parade.
I pretend I am broken.
The group leaves without me.

During the parade,
Doc Greene shows off a gas
he calls floatium.
Doc invented it to keep balloons
from floating away.

The floatium gas gets
into the lobster tank.
The lobsters start floating in the air!

Cody and Francine
think the floating lobsters are funny.
They call them flobsters!

"Oh, dear," says Doc Greene.
"The floatium will not wear off
for two more days!"
People try to jump
and catch the flobsters.

I am at home.

Kade calls me,

but I do not answer.

I am still feeling sorry for myself.

I turn on the television.
I see floating lobsters!
The flobsters attack the mayor
while he makes a speech!

The other Rescue Bots
do the best they can
to protect the humans.
I can see on TV that they still need help.

Lobsters like to eat starfish!
The flobsters think the starfish
on Francine's jacket is real.
She hides in a phone booth.

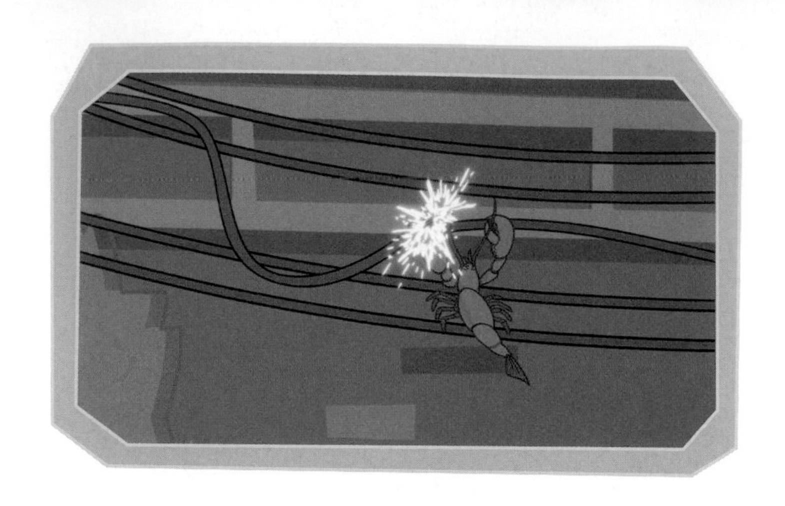

The flobsters attack!

I need to stop feeling mad.

My team needs me.

Kade needs me.

I rush into town to join the fight.
My fire hoses spray the flobsters
with massive water power.

The flobsters are afraid
of the giant lobster balloon.
We herd them into a trap
using the balloon.
I spray them back into the tank!

We saved the parade!
Everyone says
the Rescue Bots are heroes.

I feel so happy
I even let kids climb on me!
Kade whispers to me,
"You know you love it."
Guess what!
He is right!